This is my fin.
Do you have
a fin?

lip

What Do You Have?

Consultants

Ashley Bishop, Ed.D.
Sue Bishop, M.E.D.

Publishing Credits

Dona Herweck Rice, *Editor-in-Chief*
Robin Erickson, *Production Director*
Lee Aucoin, *Creative Director*
Tim J. Bradley, *Illustrator Manager*
Chad Thompson, *Illustrator*
Sharon Coan, *Project Manager*
Jamey Acosta, *Editor*
Rachelle Cracchiolo, M.A.Ed., *Publisher*

Teacher Created Materials
5301 Oceanus Drive
Huntington Beach, CA 92649-1030
http://www.tcmpub.com

ISBN 978-1-4333-2940-1

Printed in China WAI002

fin

This is my lip.
Do you have
a lip?

wig

This is my wig.
Do you have
a wig?

pin

This is my pin.
Do you have
a pin?

What do you have?

Glossary

fin

lip

pin

wig

Sight Words

This is my

Do you have

a What

Extension Activities

Read the story together with your child. Use the discussion questions before, during, and after your reading to deepen your child's understanding of the story and the rime (word family) that is introduced.

The activities provide fun ideas for continuing the conversation about the story and the vocabulary that is introduced. They will help your child make personal connections to the story and use the vocabulary to describe prior experiences.

Discussion Questions

- What is something you have that I do not?
- What is something I have that you do not?
- What is the fin in the story used for? Can you think of something else with a fin?
- What is something you use your lips for?
- What are two reasons why someone would wear a wig?

Activities at Home

- Have your child draw a picture of a pin that might be given to someone who does something brave.
- Show your child a picture of a fish and talk about how each part of the fish helps it move and breathe.